Saving Christmas Breakfast

Immortal Defiance Series
Book 2

L. S. O'Dea

I love hearing from readers.
Please contact or follow me.
www.LSODea.com

https://www.tiktok.com/@author_lsodea

https://www.bookbub.com/authors/l-s-o-dea

https://www.facebook.com/LSODeaAuthor/

Closed Lake of Sins FB Group
https://www.facebook.com/groups/137774923650964/

https://twitter.com/lsodea

Or email at lsodea7@gmail.com

Sign up for my newsletter

AND GET A FREE BOOK

HTTPS://LSODEA.COM/JOIN-THE-LAKE-OF-SINS-READERS-GROUP//

Here are some of the perks of being a member of my newsletter

- Fun and entertaining articles delivered straight to your inbox
- Group Only Giveaways
- Sneak Peeks of illustrations, book covers and stories

You can also join my closed FB group. Go here to join
https://www.facebook.com/groups/137774923650964/

Other Books by L. S. O'Dea

Read more about them on my website:
https://www.lsodea.com/

Immortal Defiance Series

This is a standalone series.
A Demon's Gift (book 1)
https://www.lsodea.com/books/a-demons-gift/
Saving Christmas Breakfast (book 2)
https://www.lsodea.com/books/saving-christmas-breakfast/

Lake of Sins Series

This series should be read in order.
FREE: Escape (book 1)
https://books2read.com/u/31xPN7

Secrets In Blood (book 2)
https://www.lsodea.com/books/secrets-in-blood/

Hangman's Army (book 3)
https://www.lsodea.com/books/hangmans-army/

Betrayed (book 4)
https://www.lsodea.com/books/betrayed/

Whispers From the Past (book 5)
https://www.lsodea.com/books/whispers-from-the-past/

Machinations and Sacrifices (book 6)
https://www.lsodea.com/books/machinations-and-sacrifices/

Lake Of Sins Box Set (books 1-3)
https://www.lsodea.com/books/lake-of-sins-box-set/

Chimera Chronicles Series
This is a standalone series.
FREE: Rise of the River Man Volume One
https://books2read.com/u/mZwWPD

Feeding Fersia – Volume Two
https://www.lsodea.com/books/feeding-fersia/

Breaking the Brush Men – Volume Three
https://www.lsodea.com/books/breaking-the-brush-men/

Rage of Rattus Norvegicus Volume Four
https://www.lsodea.com/books/rage-of-rattus-norvegicus/

Leaving Level Five Volume Five
https://www.lsodea.com/books/leaving-level-five/

Chimera Chronicles Box Set (Volumes 1-5)
https://www.lsodea.com/books/chimera-chronicles/

CHAPTER 1: Micah

Micah strode down the hospital corridor, the lights dimming to darkness as he approached. Their warmth devoured by the coldness of his presence only to flutter back to brightness as he passed. At first, he'd convinced himself that he could feel that heat for one fleeting instant, but that'd been a dream of a memory he no longer had. Angels of Death were not allowed to remember past lives. It was the first thing the gods took when they recruited the dead.

He pretended that he didn't miss the warmth of life—sunshine, a blanket, a fire. Feelings like that were for newbies. He'd been lectured for centuries to stop wanting things he couldn't have and to accept his existence as it was. No pain. No torment. No decisions. Nothing but darkness and death.

He didn't need to glance at the number on the rooms to know where he was to be. The sorrow echoed down the hallway, leading him to his destination. He stopped in the doorway. It was almost time.

Two adults slept with their hands clasped. Their love bound them tighter for their troubles. Other children rested. Their minds were uneasy, but exhaustion had won this war. A boy lay in the bed, drifting between the world of the living and Micah's realm.

The young seemed to be rushing to his world too soon lately—drugs, alcohol, suicide—but not this one. This child had the scent and look of one who'd suffered for years. Why had Gillstrom sent him to collect this spirit? His boss knew he hated taking children—so much life untapped, so much warmth not given. Other Angels enjoyed taking the sick, no matter the age. They believed they brought peace from the pain, but all he saw was the end of a life before it'd had a chance to live.

He slipped into the room and leaned against the wall. It didn't matter what he thought. Old. Young. Healthy. Sick. His job was to escort them to the next part of their journey whether he liked it or not.

CHAPTER 2: Bobby

Bobby was dying. He had been since birth or at least as far back in his twelve years that he could remember. Leukemia. The hated "L" word. He'd been fighting it forever, but it'd finally won. His battle was almost over.

He turned his head, careful not to wake his mother who was curled up in the hospital bed with him. The nurses had stopped telling her it wasn't allowed days ago. His father dozed in the chair, even in sleep he held his wife's hand, sharing strength and sorrow. Ricky was curled up on their father's lap, ten years old and never sick a day. His little brother was the complete opposite of him. It sucked that the kid had to spend Christmas in the hospital instead of playing in the snow and opening presents. Beth, his fifteen-year-old sister, slept in a chair near his oldest brother who was the only one still awake.

Nick sat by the bed, clutching Bobby's hand and talking in hushed whispers. Bobby could barely comprehend the words anymore, only the feelings—fear, desperation, anger, love. He understood because he felt them all too. His life had been short and hard, cruel even and it wasn't fair. He wanted to shout at God, but He wasn't here, so his messenger would have to do.

CHAPTER 3: Bobby

Bobby turned away from his brother and focused on the corner where the light refused to enter. "You can come out. I know you're there." His words were more thought than sound as his body slowly surrendered to its fate.

"I was waiting for you." The shadows shifted, consuming the brightness as the dark angel stepped into the open.

"Why?" It was one word, but it held so many questions. Why him? Why now? Why? Rage, an emotion he hadn't felt in a long time, roared through him. "Why?" He almost sobbed. He didn't want to die. He'd barely lived.

"It's what must be." The words were soft but almost echoed in the room as the Angel moved closer. He was beautiful with black eyes in a pale face, dark hair that fell to his shoulders and clothes so black that they devoured the light.

"It's not fair." It was a stupid plea, but it was the truth. He'd suffered so much. His family had suffered so much.

"It's what must be," repeated the Angel as he stopped at the bed, bringing with him a murky shadow that promised something besides pain. "Come." He held out his hand.

"No. Please." He wasn't ready. His fingers squeezed his brother's, clinging to the golden warmth of life.

"It's time." The Angel opened his arms, beckoning.

"Please. One more Christmas. One more Christmas breakfast. We've never had one Christmas without worry. One where Mom didn't pretend her tears were because she was happy."

She'd always put on a brave face and for moments he'd forget the sorrow that he'd caused her, but then she'd disappear, and his father and older siblings would get extra happy. It was as false as his hope of getting better.

"It's all I want. Just one Christmas breakfast. Can't I have that? Can't we have that? Please, give us one Christmas morning that we should've had. One where I wasn't sick. Where I'd never been sick." Tears streamed down his cheeks. His family deserved that. He deserved that.

The Angel studied him, black eyes seeing into his soul. "I am allowed one miracle."

"Pick me." His heart raced, and hope fluttered to life, bringing him strength. "Please." He touched his mother's hair, soft and still slightly fragrant from her shower that morning. "They deserve it. She deserves it."

"There is no undoing this once it's done."

"Undoing?" He'd never ask that. "No. Of course. Just

6

let us keep the memory."

"Not memory. Life. You'll be well." The Angel's face was grave.

His brain froze like he'd eaten ice cream too fast. He couldn't even fathom not being sick.

"Things will be different." The Angel frowned down at him. "I cannot tell you what your life will be like, but it'll be different than what you think it'll be."

"I don't care." He knew it wouldn't be perfect, but he'd get to live, really live. He'd play baseball and go back to school. He'd run track and play in the rain. There was so much he'd never been able to do, and he'd do it all.

"Are you sure?"

"Yes. I'm sure," he shouted, but his family didn't move. This conversation was still beyond their ears.

"I'm going to say this again." The intensity in the Angel's eyes made him squirm. "Once this is done, there is no going back."

"I understand." He'd never want to go back to being sick and being the reason his mom and dad cried, and their home filled with sadness.

"Close your eyes." The Angel's hand lowered toward his face, blocking the light as if it'd never existed.

CHAPTER 4: Micah

Micah covered the boy's eyes. The kid was right. He deserved a life without pain. Unfortunately, that didn't exist. Humans never understood how one small change can alter fate, and illness and death were not small things.

Yet, he was given one miracle a year, and he'd been punished before for not using it. He probably wouldn't find another as deserving. His lips turned up in a sneer. Deserving. Ha. The kid should get more than a twisted miracle, but those who churned fate had a sick sense of humor. Miracles were never free, and someone would pay dearly for this one.

CHAPTER 5: Bobby

A chill seeped into Bobby from the Angel's hand. At first, it was like a fresh, cool blanket, but soon it grew frigid and uncomfortable. He tried to move, to get away from the Angel's touch, but the being's fingers elongated, filling his body with cold that sparked like a thousand matches. He opened his mouth to cry out but then there was nothing. No pain. No weakness. No exhaustion.

His breath came easy now and his limbs felt light. He opened his eyes. He was in his bed. In his house. He felt…good. Wonderful. He sat up, careful not to bump his head on the top bunk, but it wasn't there.

"Ricky?" He crawled out of bed. Everything was different. He was taller and heavier—his hair thick and his skin warm. The room was filled with toys—baseballs, basketballs, and action figures. His clothes littered the floor. Mom would never allow this. "Ricky?"

He scanned the room again, the small nightlight sending a soft glow through the darkness but stopping at a corner. A shadow lurked there, eating the light.

"Where's my brother?"

"There is no Ricky." The Angel moved toward him, the light disappearing as he walked.

"What do you mean by that?" Coldness, even more frigid than the Angel's hand, filled him.

"Without your sickness there was no sorrow. No need for comfort in the night. Your parents never had another child after you."

"Oh." Sadness filled him for the loss of a brother he'd never had.

"You'll forget soon," said the Angel. "The memories of what was, will be replaced by memories of what is."

"Where is he? Was he born to someone else? Is he happy?"

"His soul is in another body. As to the other, I cannot say."

"You can't say?" His parents used sneaky words like those when they didn't want to tell him the truth about what the doctors said. "But you know."

The Angel nodded.

"Tell me. I don't want my…my decision, my life to cause him to suffer. He's not sick, is he?"

"I cannot tell you. Everything that happens from here on out will be your memory."

"Please."

"It isn't allowed."

"You said I'll forget everything that was. That means you too, right?"

"Yes." The Angel eyed him suspiciously.

"Then tell me about Ricky now. It doesn't count because I'll forget it anyway."

The Angel sighed, but his lips tipped upward in a slight smile. "I suppose it won't hurt anything. He is well. He is loved and healthy. You may even meet him one day."

"Thank you. Thank you." He wrapped his arms around the being, surprised that the creature was more than mist and prayer.

"Do not thank me." The Angel stiffened and stepped away. "I must go. I shouldn't be here now." He tipped his head. "I have others to visit today."

"Thank…Merry Christm…" He paused as the being disappeared. He scanned the room, but the light filled every corner, not bending away from even the tiniest space. "Thank you," he whispered.

The Angel may not want to hear it, but he was going to say it anyway. It was Christmas. He was well. His little brother was safe, and he'd see him again one day. Life was good. He ran from his bedroom. The house was quiet. He was the first to wake, but he'd get the others up. The day was too wonderful to sleep.

CHAPTER 6: Bobby

Bobby raced down the hallway, slapping his hand on Beth's door as he passed. "Wake up. It's Christmas and I'm not sick." He pushed into his brother's room. "Nick. Nick, wake up." He skidded to a stop. The room was empty. The bed was still made. Nick had probably worked late and was now in the kitchen with their parents cooking breakfast.

His stomach rumbled. He was starving. He'd never been this hungry in his entire life. He continued down the hallway, stopping in the living room. The tree was lit, chasing away the dark. Beth sat on the couch, phone to her ear, whispering.

"Merry Christmas." He grinned at his sister.

"Yeah, Merry Christmas." She didn't even look at him.

"Where is everyone?" The kitchen was dark. An almost empty wine bottle sat on the table next to a single glass.

"How should I know?" She still didn't look at him.

"Why aren't they making breakfast?" His parents were

always the first ones up on Christmas.

"What are you talking about?" She glanced at him, a disgusted look on her face.

"Christmas breakfast." He wanted to say "duh". How could Beth forget that? They did it every year. It was a huge spread—eggs, bacon, pancakes, everything.

"What's wrong with you?" She stared at him like he'd grown another head.

"Nothing. Nothing at all." He spread his arms wide and then jumped into the air. "I'm not sick. Not even a little."

"Well, goodie for you." She rolled her eyes.

He laughed. She didn't remember, but he still did. He'd done his best to pretend to feel good for them, but now he felt like he could run a hundred miles, climb the highest tree, and swim the ocean. His stomach rumbled again. Breakfast first and then…He climbed over his sister and pulled the curtains apart.

"Hey, get off me." She shoved him.

"It snowed." He ignored her, nothing would stop him, not today. "Look at all that snow." He'd seen it before from his bed, but today he'd get to go out and play for hours. His parents had let him play in the snow before but only for a little while and they'd watched him like he was going to die any minute.

They'd kept him busy with hot chocolate and movies or games while his siblings had spent hours outside sledding and making forts. He'd never said anything because he'd understood, but today…nothing would stop him from playing outside until he almost passed out. He

13

was strong now; he wasn't sick. Mom wouldn't have to try and hide her worry.

"Mom." He pulled his eyes away from the window. His sister had given up fighting with him and had squeezed into the corner of the couch, her phone still glued to her ear. "Where is she?"

"In bed. Where else?" Beth turned her back to him as she continued talking on the phone.

He should let his mother sleep, but he couldn't. He wanted her to see him. To see how healthy he was. "Mom! Dad!" He ran to their bedroom. "It's Christmas. Wake-up." He threw open the door. "You have to make breakfast. I'm starving."

"What?" His mom rolled over and then sat up. "What's the matter, Bobby."

"Nothing." Suddenly, it all hit him, and his eyes filled with tears as he inhaled, having trouble believing he was actually well. "I…I'm not sick." He ran across the room, wrapping his arms around his mother. "I'm not sick, Mom. Not at all." He sobbed, relief washing through him, cleansing him of the worry that'd been a part of him for as long as he could remember.

"Oh, honey." She hugged him. "I'm glad." She kissed his head. "Are you okay?" She pulled back, looking at him.

"Yeah." He nodded, wiping his eyes. "I feel great. Hungry. Starving." Those words should've put a smile on her face that couldn't be wiped away, but she just nodded.

"Okay. Let's get you something." She got out of bed. "Although, you're old enough to make your own

14

breakfast."

"Yeah, but this is Christmas." He grabbed her hand, tugging her toward the kitchen.

"So?" She pulled on her robe.

"We all cook. You and Dad make sausage and pancakes, and me and Ric...I set the table and pick out the music. Beth squeezes the oranges after Nick cuts them for her."

"What are you talking about?" She shot him a glare as she headed into the kitchen.

He glanced at the empty bed. "Where's Dad?"

"Stop it, Bobby. It's not funny." Mom took a pack of bagels out of the fridge. "Do you want one or two?"

"Not bagels. Pancakes." This wasn't right.

Nothing was the same. The table was smaller with four chairs instead of six, and even though they only ate fast food on special occasions, a bunch of takeout containers filled the garbage.

"Fine." She put the bagels back in the refrigerator and pulled a package of frozen pancakes from the freezer. "How many?"

"Not frozen. Dad makes them from scratch." He didn't understand what was going on. They should all be in here making Christmas breakfast.

"Then you'll have to wait for him to pick you up"— she threw the pancakes back into the freezer—"if he even bothers. He's probably too busy with his new girlfriend," she muttered as she headed for her bedroom.

Girlfriend? "What? Where are you going?"

15

"To change." She slammed the door.

Beth walked into the kitchen, bumping into him on purpose as she moved to the fridge. "Nice going." She pulled out the carton of orange juice. "Why are you bringing *him* up anyway?"

"Him? Who?" He was so confused. It was like they were all strangers who looked like his family.

"Exactly. I bet he doesn't even call us." She poured OJ into a glass.

"Who?"

"Dad, you moron." She put the juice back into the fridge.

The phone rang and Mom came out of her bedroom. "It's your father." She held out her cell. "He's going to cancel on picking you up for Christmas. Again."

"Big surprise," snorted Beth as she walked past her mother, ignoring the phone.

"Hey, it's not like that," said Dad.

"Really?" Mom put the phone by her ear. "Then exactly what is it like? This will be the third Christmas you haven't bothered to see your kids." She paused as Dad said something, her face twisting with disgust. "They don't want money. They want their father." Her phone beeped. "Hold on. Someone's calling." She looked at the screen and pressed a button, before putting the phone back to her ear. "Hello. Yes, this is Mrs. Lazetti." She turned her back to Bobby. "No. That's not possible. He's here. In bed. I'm sure." She hurried out of the room and came back a few moments later, her face pinched with worry. "Where's your

16

brother?"

"I don't know." He shrugged. "Nick wasn't in his room when I got up."

Her arm trembled as she put the phone back to her ear. "I...I...Where?" She leaned against the counter, one hand clinging to it as if it were the only thing keeping her from falling to the floor. "I'll...I'll be there as soon as I can." She hung up the phone, her face white and her eyes darting around as if in panic.

"What's wrong?" Beth stood in the kitchen doorway. "Mom, who was that?"

"I...Your father." She pressed a button. "Greg...Shut up. I don't care why you aren't coming over." Her voice cracked. "That was the hospital. Nick's been in an accident."

CHAPTER 7: Bobby

Bobby followed his mother and sister into the hospital. They stopped at a counter and his mother spoke to the woman there.

The Angel had said he'd forget everything about his past…his other life…but he didn't think he'd ever forget the hospital. He'd spent so much time here, almost his entire life, but unlike his home, this place hadn't changed. It was still cold and clean. The white walls and tile floors worked with the bright lights, trying to keep death away, but it never worked. Death would enter, eating the light and leaving only sorrow and darkness.

They walked down a hallway and got into an elevator. It was familiar but different. He wasn't sick but the worry was still on his mom's face. The doors opened and they stepped out into another corridor almost identical to the one they'd just left. They turned and headed into a waiting room.

"Dad!" He raced toward his father who sat on a chair

18

next to a young woman.

"Bobby." Dad stood, opening his arms.

"Dad," he sobbed against his father's chest. He was well but he'd never wanted this. It wasn't fair. The Angel hadn't told him this would happen.

"Hey, it's going to be okay." Dad squeezed him tightly. "It is. You'll see."

"What did they say?" Mom stood to the side.

"Not much." Dad stepped away from Bobby and the younger woman immediately took his father's hand.

"What happened?" Mom's lips pinched even more as her eyes darted to the other woman.

"He was drinking and driving."

"No." She dropped onto the closest chair. "I told him to call me. No matter the time."

"I did too," said Dad.

A doctor in blue scrubs walked toward them. Her face was tired, and her eyes were filled with sorrow. Bobby knew that look. The doctors had worn that same expression every time his leukemia had come back. Sometimes they'd smiled, trying to ease his worry, but their eyes had always told the truth. His parents stood like statues as the doctor approached, waiting for the news that'd ruin their lives.

"No," he whispered. He couldn't let this happen. He looked around, in every corner and at every shadow, but there was nothing but white walls and light. The Angel was here somewhere. He had to be.

Bobby stumbled away from his parents, looking everywhere—the hallway, behind the chairs, in every corner—for the darkness in the light. A tiny shadow moved down the corridor like a thief, stealing the bright whiteness of the lights, walls and floor.

"Wait! Stop!" He ran down the hallway.

The shadow moved faster in the other direction.

"Hey, young man. You can't…"

Bobby ignored the nurse, darting around her. "I didn't want this. You should've told me. You tricked me."

The shadow stopped, turning and growing into the Angel as it consumed all light around them. Everyone else continued to go about their business as if neither of them was there.

"I told you that it'd be different." The Angel's dark eyes were hard like obsidian.

"You never said it'd be like this. Mom and Dad not together. Ricky gone. Nick…" His voice cracked. Nick had been his best friend. His brother had always been there to play with him, to sneak him candy and to tell him about shows he wasn't allowed to stay up and watch. "It's not what I wanted."

"It is what you asked." The darkness around the Angel grew even blacker like the sky before a storm. "You wanted to be well. You're well."

"Yeah, but…" He glanced over his shoulder.

His father hugged the young woman. His sister stood away from their parents, crying and talking into her phone, while his mother sat frozen and alone on a chair. Her face was so tight the soft breeze from someone walking by might make her shatter into a million pieces.

"I didn't want this. It's not a miracle. It's a nightmare." He sobbed. "You tricked me."

"I did not trick you." The Angel's dark eyes glowed red with fury.

CHAPTER 8: Micah

Micah glared at the boy. This was why he hated these miracles. They always had a price, but this time someone screwed up. The kid should've forgotten everything by now.

"Y-you did trick me. I never asked to be well forever." Bobby's small chin jutted out stubbornly. "All I wanted was not to be sick for one Christmas breakfast so no one would worry about me."

"And I gave you that. You'll have many Christmas breakfasts like that."

"I don't want them like this." Tears forged a trail down the child's cheeks. "I wanted a Christmas breakfast like we had before."

"I cannot undo what was done. I explained that."

"But...but this wasn't what I wanted." He wiped his nose with his shirtsleeve.

"I'm sorry. There is nothing I can do." He hated his job. He hated the unending sorrow. Even when the soul was old and in pain, the grief of the family, friends or the nurses and doctors tainted the room.

"Pl-please. I never asked you for this. There has to be a way…a rule. You didn't give me the miracle that I asked for. You gave me some—"

"I gave you life." Micah's words burned like fire. "I gave you health." He wasn't taking the blame for this. He could hear the bells of trouble ringing already—soft, ominous chimes notifying him to see his superior when he was done with his assignment.

"I-I never asked you for that. I wanted one breakfast. That's all."

The sorrow in the child's eyes was so deep Micah felt as if he were being pulled into the depths, drowning in dark, never-ending waves of misery. This was the kind of pain that never went away. Somehow, he understood this agony, but that was impossible. He had no memory of life, but impossible or not, he knew this.

"Please." Bobby's gaze moved to the room where his brother's soul waited to be collected. "Save him. Take me instead." The boy clasped Micah's hand.

A flicker of memory fluttered through him. He wasn't sure if it were the words or something in the child's touch, but he'd done this before. He'd sacrificed…No. Maybe. He wasn't sure. Had he sacrificed himself like Bobby was doing or had he failed? Micah closed his eyes, trying to remember his past, his life, but the memories were surrounded by shadow.

"Please, Mr. Angel. Save my family."

"I cannot." He pulled his hand from the boy's grasp. He'd be punished if he did this. Gillstrom already didn't like him.

"You promised. You said you'd save Christmas breakfast."

"I did. You'll have years of Christmas breakfasts."

"No. I'll have breakfast on Christmas but that's not the same as Christmas breakfast. They aren't a family, not really." The boy glanced down the hallway. "My mom's alone. My dad is unhappy. My sister…Ricky…They'll never have each other and…" He swallowed. "Nick. Nick will be…" His small jaw stiffened. "I asked you to save Christmas breakfast. You agreed but you didn't do it."

"Are you threatening me?" He had to admit, he was amused.

"No." The boy's eyes sharpened. "I just want you to honor our deal."

"You'll die."

"I don't care. Nick will live." The child's face scrunched up in distrust. "Right? Nick will be fine if I…if I go back to how it was."

"Yes. Your brother will be fine, and you'll be dead." He didn't want to take this child. The boy had heart and loyalty. The world needed people like him.

"Promise?"

"Yes." He almost smiled. He didn't blame Bobby for his distrust. The whole miracle thing was always slippery.

The boy took a deep breath. "Then do it." His eyes met the Angel's again. "Please." Bobby tipped back his head, placing the Angel's hand over his eyes. "Please. Save Christmas breakfast for my family."

He shouldn't. He really shouldn't but something about this boy, this situation…He couldn't explain it, but he also couldn't walk away. "Close your eyes."

CHAPTER 9: Bobby

Bobby trembled as pain, white hot and intense, flooded his body. His mouth opened to cry out but snapped shut as the suffocating dullness of the drugs flowed through him, taking away the hurt. His eyes fluttered open.

"He's awake." Mom stood by the bed. She squeezed his hand, leaning down and kissing his forehead. "Hey, little man."

"Mom." He tried to tighten his fingers around hers, yearning for the warmth, the connection, but his hand wouldn't obey.

"Hey, champ." Dad stood next to Mom, his arm around her.

Beth was at the foot of the bed, his little brother clasped onto her side, tears streaming down his round cheeks.

"Ricky, you're here."

"Ye…yes. I'm not going anywhere." Ricky wiped his face on his sister's shirt, but she only tightened her arms around him.

"Beth." He smiled at her. "No…phone?" The words were getting harder and harder to form as he slowly slid away from this world.

"What?" She glanced at their parents, confusion on her pretty face.

He was too tired to explain, and it didn't matter. Nothing mattered except that they were together. A family. The Angel hovered closer, his darkness stealing all the light, but no one besides Bobby seemed to notice.

"Wait. Not yet. Please." He tried to sit up, but his body failed him. "Nick? Where's Nick."

"I'm right here, buddy." His older brother stood on the other side of his bed. Nick quickly wiped his eyes and then clasped Bobby's hand.

He glanced at the Angel who stood to his brother's side. "Thank you."

"For what, kiddo?" asked Nick.

The Angel nodded and held out his hand. "It's time."

"One minute. Please." He didn't want to go. His fingers trembled as he tried to tighten his hold on his brother's and mother's hands.

"I'm here, buddy." Nick squatted so he was face level with Bobby. "As long as you like."

"Stay. To…gether." His words were barely a whisper.

The Angel's hand moved closer, sliding through Nick's and taking Bobby's, replacing his brother's warmth with coldness.

CHAPTER 10: Micah

Micah was going to be in trouble for this, but he was sick of miracles that were nothing but tricks. They hadn't even given the kid time to forget. He still wasn't sure how that'd happened. Usually, they forgot as soon as they opened their eyes, but Bobby hadn't.

He'd promised the boy a miracle and he was going to give him one. He'd deal with the consequences later. Amusement sparked inside him—warm but fleeting, like a match struck and then doused in water. He could almost see Gillstrom now. The other angel was like a pulsing nerve, sparking on about the rules and regulations. This just might make Gillstrom twitch himself out of existence. If only Micah would be so lucky.

"I'm scared." The boy hadn't spoken but Micah could feel his thoughts.

Death shimmered around the child's body. When he'd first taken this job, he'd imagined death to be a dark nothingness, but it was white hot and sharp like ice covered snow in the sunshine. It filled the body with shards until the soft flesh couldn't take anymore and exploded, pushing the energy that was life back into the universe.

"It'll be okay," he whispered even though no one but the child could hear him. "I promise. You'll be better soon."

"No. Nick." The child used the little strength he had to squeeze his brother's hand.

"Shhh. Your brother will be fine. Your family will be fine too." He, on the other hand, would pay for this.

Another memory lurched out of the shadows—a man strode across a field, his eyes hard with determination and his jaw tight with stubbornness. Then it disappeared as quickly as it came, but the feelings remained. It'd been him. He had no idea where he'd been going but he'd been scared. Terrified. Yet, he'd continued onward, too stubborn to stop. Apparently, an eternity of collecting the sorrows of souls hadn't changed him much.

His hands glided over the boy's face and down his body. Normally, he drew the soul to him, his touch like a magnet helping them leave the white-hot pain, but this time he pushed it back. "Stay." Leaving the soul in this body wouldn't be enough. Bobby would die. He had to collect the death.

His fingers scraped along the child's tiny frame, gathering the icy shards of death. His body brightened and trembled as Death entered him. He gasped at the feeling. He hadn't expected this to hurt. He hadn't felt anything but sorrow and emptiness for years.

Another shard sprang from Bobby and into Micah's hand. It broke through the cold and darkness, making his essence burn. This wasn't going to be fun. He had a lot more death to collect. He braced himself as he leaned into the body.

The shell that was the boy gasped, his breath foul with the pungent scent of the dying. Bobby's body jerked. Death had a firm grip on this child, and it didn't want to let go of its prize. Bobby cried out, a sheer sound of torment. Micah had to make this quick or the kid would never survive. The child was weak from his lifetime battle.

"Dad! Mom!" Nick stared in horror as his brother's body convulsed.

"Help! Doctor! Nurse! Someone!" The father ran out of the door and into the hallway. "We need help. A doctor. Please. Someone, help us!"

The nurses piled into the room, rushing to the bed and moving the family away from the boy. The sister held her little brother tighter as her other arm reached out to Nick. The mother and father clung to each other, their fear filling the room with a sweet scent.

They had reason to fear. Death wound tight through the organs and the cells of the child, making itself at home.

Bobby convulsed again, his mouth opening on a silent scream, but Micah heard the sound. It was so loud it reverberated through his body, making the lights in the room flicker in warning. This battle between him and Death waged strong, but he'd win because he'd never give up. Gillstrom and those above him had to know what he was doing. It may get him a one-way ticket to toil and torment, but he'd rather be damned for success than failure. He dug in deeper, his body almost disappearing into the child.

The nurses and doctors brushed through him as they moved around the room, giving him the sweet warmth of life for a fraction of a second. He swayed toward them, trying to gather whatever heat he could in order to offset the icy burn of death that shot into him like bullets as it left the child.

The doctor shouted to increase the morphine as Bobby's body continued to convulse. Micah's shadowy form pulsed and throbbed every time the boy twitched. Death tore through them both, ripping them apart. It snapped and chewed, angry and alive as it ate its way up his arms. It roared into him in force. It'd found a new victim. Death hunted him now, not the boy, but he needed to move before Death realized he was a shell of a meal. He threw himself away from the child.

Bobby almost lifted off the bed as Death ripped free from his body and leapt for Micah, shooting into the room like a window imploding. The shards of icy glass hung in the air, shifting back and forth as if looking for a place to land. Micah wanted to hide in the shadows until Death found a new host, but he'd promised. He couldn't let it make a home in someone else.

The icy spikes tinkled like a giant deadly chandelier as Death searched the room. Micah's knees shook. This was going to hurt. He flung his arms wide and called to Death, his companion, his enemy, his job.

In a flash it obeyed, slamming into him like bullets from a machine gun. His body jerked with each explosion of pain. The equipment in the room beeped incessantly and the lights turned off and on as he staggered backward, hitting the wall with his arms outstretched as if crucified.

Another memory jumped from the shadows of his mind. That same man…him…on the ground, dirty and beaten. His arms stretched wide. Tied to something. He snorted back a panicked laugh. It seemed fitting that his eternal life end similar to the way his earthly life had.

The shards continued to shoot into him, one after the other, until he cried out in anguish. He'd forgotten so much about life. He'd missed so much, but not this. Not this pain. His body convulsed with each hit until his legs gave out and he crumpled to the floor and then it was done. Death was gone. The lights glowed softly in the room, except near him where darkness fell. He breathed deeply, once again feeling nothing but coldness.

The family huddled together, sobs breaking the sharp hum of the flatline. The boy lay still in the bed, no breath lifting his chest.

CHAPTER 11: Micah

Micah waited…and waited. He'd never done this before, but there was no way he'd failed. Death was gone. He'd taken it. He looked around. There were no other angels here. Was he to take the boy even after trying to save him? He wouldn't put it past his superiors. They followed a different agenda—one without mercy.

A beep echoed through the quiet room, quickly followed by another and another.

Micah didn't move, as frozen as the family as they all watched the boy in the bed. Bobby's eyes fluttered, an almost imperceptible movement and then they opened. Suddenly, the room burst with energy. The doctors and nurses moved about the bed checking the boy's vitals. The family sobbed tears of joy tainted with unease. They didn't know that Bobby was better. No one knew but him…and his bosses.

"I can't see you." The boy's eyes searched the room, his lips moving without sound. "Where did you go?"

Only a few moments—fractions of seconds—remained before the boy would forget. Micah wanted to say goodbye. He'd saved this life. No tricks. No twisting of words and promises. "I'm right here."

Bobby's eyes drifted away from the corners and toward his family as the doctor and nurses stepped aside. It was too late. The boy was in the land of the living and could no longer hear him.

"What happened? Is he going to be okay?" The mother's eyes dimmed, thinking her question was ill-formed—still believing her son was dying.

"We should talk," said the doctor. "Outside."

"Mom, I'm hungry." Bobby leaned up slightly, a tint of color on his cheeks. The blood moved fast in the healthy. "It's Christmas. We have to have Christmas breakfast."

The father's laughter broke into a sob for one long second and then he cleared his throat. "Yes. We will. Of course, we will." He hugged his son.

"Anything you want." The mother took the father's place, holding her child to her chest. "What are you hungry for."

"Everything." Bobby leaned away from her, his eyes bright and without pain. "I'm starving.

"Please. Mr. and Mrs. Lazetti, let's talk outside." The doctor waited by the door.

"We'll be right back." The father took his wife's hand, and they both moved slowly across the room, glancing back at their child as if it'd be the last time they'd see him.

Micah didn't need to listen to know that the doctor

would fill them with dire news, explaining that sometimes a person seemed better before the end. Soon the tests would show that this wasn't the end. It was the beginning of Bobby's healthy life. The doctors and nurses would mark it down as a miracle, but they'd talk. There'd be whispers in the back rooms about the lights and machines, and Micah would be punished for that as well. True miracles caused too many questions.

The two brothers and sister surrounded the bed, talking and laughing. Bobby glanced around one more time, his eyes sharp. The boy couldn't remember, could he?

The child's eyes drifted past Micah and then back. They were unfocused, taking in the area and not the Angel. "Thank you for saving Christmas breakfast. We'll make this one special, and I'll never forget what you did for my family."

"You're welcome." He didn't think the child could hear him, His words only existed in the realm between the living and the dead, but he couldn't stop himself from reaching out, from trying. The child thought he was still ill. That the gift was one more day. One pain free Christmas breakfast. "You'll have many but make them all count."

"Who are you talking to?" asked Nick.

"No one. I mean"—Bobby smiled and the warmth of that smile heated Micah's soul—"a friend."

"A friend?" Nick looked into the corner where his brother stared, his eyes seeing nothing but wall and shadowed light. "What friend?"

"A really good one." Bobby's grin widened. "The best

friend I ever had."

The warmth that filled Micah was almost uncomfortable after centuries of cold nothingness. He wanted to reassure Bobby that he was better, but the boy couldn't hear him any longer. He'd find out soon enough that he had a lifetime of Christmas breakfasts with his family.

Micah glided from the room. The doctor spoke in hushed tones, telling the parents that their son feeling better would probably only last a little while. He explained that they should appreciate this time but to prepare for the end. That was good advice for everyone, even those like Bobby who wouldn't be sick for years to come.

His gaze drifted to the end of the hallway where a dark shadow devoured the light…except for a few sparkles that seemed oblivious to Gillstrom's presence. This wasn't good. His boss had brought a Binder with him. He was in more trouble than he'd thought, but there was no escape. He strode forward. He'd made a choice and it was time to pay because all miracles had a cost.

Thanks for reading *Saving Christmas Breakfast* I hope you enjoyed the story.

For a limited time, you can get the original story Saving Christmas Breakfast (original ending) for free (https://dl.bookfunnel.com/82lwg6no10) when you sign up for my newsletter. This story has a different ending than the one you just read.

And don't forget to check out the excerpts below. In *A Demon's Gift*, you'll learn more about the Binders and the spirits and gods of this series.

You can also sign up for my newsletter and get a free book (Secrets in Blood) from the Lake of Sins series.

HTTPS://LSODEA.COM/JOIN-THE-LAKE-OF-SINS-READERS-GROUP//

You can also join my closed FB group.

https://www.facebook.com/groups/137774923650964/

A Demon's Gift

Every inch of Iatee's body pressed against something soft and fuzzy. He tried to wiggle but his limbs didn't obey. That could mean only one thing, the gods had not been satisfied with the progress he'd made in his last life and he was once again inanimate. Whatever type of container his new body was stuffed into lifted off the ground, causing him to shift but not enough to enable him to see. Footsteps plodded on something hard, transporting him somewhere.

"You. What's your name?"

There was no sound but Iatee heard the question. Another spirit was here. He'd encountered others like him several times in the years of his imprisonment but not in a long, long time. "I am Iatee. Who are you?"

"Nongulous. How long have you been a prisoner?"

"Forever." At least, it felt like that.

"Forever? Now, that is a long time." Nongulous laughed, the sound rich and melodious.

"It is if one is a toy. Animal is not so bad, but a toy is…excruciating." The endless days of nothing grated on his soul but even that was better than being played with—mauled by sticky fingers and snotty faces. He would've shivered if he'd had any muscles.

"You were an animal? What kind? I'd love to be a monkey or a squirrel."

"I was many." The memories flickered through his mind—the freedom, the hunger, the hunt.

"Like what?"

"A seal. Penguin. Buffalo. A lion." It'd gone downhill from there. The gods were disgusted with his refusal to conform and each iteration of life became a lower and lower form.

"You got to swim in the ocean? That'd be so amazing. What was it like?"

"It was good. Vast open waters. Swimming for hours and hours." He'd loved the freedom and the hunt, chasing the fish, catching them with his teeth and tearing into them. It'd been glorious, except for the young. The mating had been grand but he hadn't liked going back to land to care for his offspring. So, he hadn't. The gods had not liked that.

"And a lion. Did you kill a lot?" Envy and longing filled Nongulous' voice.

"I killed everything I found." Including his own kind and their young—again, behavior no longer pleasing to the gods.

"I wish they would've let me be an animal instead of sticking me right into toy-terror."

"Toy-terror?" Iatee chuckled. "That's an apt description of this torture." It was also an accurate account of his first time as a toy.

His spirit had been imprisoned inside a board game. He'd despised it—the pounding of the pieces as they moved over his body and the grubby little hands, pressing down on him—until he'd learned to control his wheel. He'd made sure the snot-faced boy who'd *owned* him had never won again.

No one *owned* Iatee. He was a Punishment Spirit. Born when the earth was fresh and the gods were hungry. He'd been created to hunt and to punish. He'd been celebrated, feared and revered. His victories were legends remembered through song, but no one would be singing about his triumph over the child. The boy had tired of losing and had quit playing with him. His life as a toy had never been better until he'd been given away like trash. He'd lingered on a shelf, being mauled and molested—pieces falling out and getting lost—losing himself bit by bit until he'd been incinerated.

"This is my third time," said Nongulous. "What about you?"

"More than I can count." He'd been trapped in one form or another for so long that his real life seemed only a dream.

"Oh Iatee, what did you do to deserve a punishment like that? Even one lifetime as a toy feels like eternity."

"I did nothing except what I was created to do. I hunted. I punished. I killed."

"That's not good. The gods don't like that anymore."

"The gods cannot change. It's not right."

"Right or not…there's no room for a demon in this world. The gods know that and adjusted. We either change with them or suffer."

"I am not a demon." He almost spat the word. "That's a human term. I'm a Punishment Spirit. The gods created me as I am. I did their bidding. No matter what they asked. Punishment. Plague. Slaughter. I did what they told me and they…they turned me into this." He couldn't hide his vehemence. It was a fast, hot feeling that burned through him. He'd killed many over the years but he'd never hated until his imprisonment.

The person carrying the box stilled as if feeling Iatee's rage.

"Shhh. You must be quiet. Humans cannot know we exist. It's against the rules." Nongulous' thoughts whispered through Iatee's head.

"They aren't my rules. They've never been my rules and Iatee will not change." But he did stop talking. If they were discovered, it'd mean another transformation. Since the gods would blame them, it meant the next form would be worse than whatever this one was.

"Everything okay?" yelled a man from a distance.

"I think there's something in here." The man carrying them shook the box.

"Are you sure?" The other man walked toward them. "And listen very closely before you answer." His footsteps stopped nearby. "If there are rats or mice in these boxes we're going to have to search them. Every stinking one of them. You know what that means? To make our quota we'll have to stay late."

"I can't stay tonight. I have to pick up my kid."

"Then, you get fired but only if there's something in there." The man tapped the box. "Understand?"

"Ah…yes, sir."

"So, is there anything wrong?"

"No, sir. Nothing." The man took a few steps and the box flew through the air, dropping onto something solid.

Iatee fell forward. Great. Now, he was almost upside down.

"Thanks, so much," whispered Nongulous. "My face is in some stuffed animal's ass."

"Stuffed animal? We're stuffed animals?"

"Yes and shut up," Nongulous whispered. "We can't talk now."

That was fine with him. His dream had finally been answered. He was a stuffed animal. The gods were giving him another chance.

Find out what happens next.

https://www.lsodea.com/books/a-demons-gift/

Free ebook - Lake of Sins: Escape

Book 1 of the Lake of Sins series. (excerpt)

Trinity trudged through the forest. The sun's strong rays blinded her as she walked and her feet ached. Her stomach rumbled. She'd eat when she stopped for the night. Hunger was nothing new to her. She shifted the backpack on her shoulders and trudged around a bend. A flash caught her eye. Something silver glistened on the rocks, sparkling like ice crystals in the sunshine. It was partially submerged in the water. She cautiously approached, ready to run into the forest at any sign of danger. It was similar to her in size and shape except instead of feet and hands this creature had flippers and a long, thick tail. Its skin was silver-gray and scaly. It was hairless and lying on its side with its head in the water. There were four slits along its rib cage.

"Hey, are you all right?" She took a couple of steps back in case it was just sleeping.

The creature didn't move. She should just go. She didn't have time for this, but she'd never seen anything like it. She crept closer, her heart beating faster with each step. Her feet were in the water now. She was only a few feet away. She nudged it with the bottom of the stick and jumped back. It remained still, lifeless. She moved farther into the water and poked it again, harder this time. There was still no reaction. It was dead. *Poor, ugly thing.* What had happened to it? Had it drowned? It kind of looked like a fish. Maybe, it suffocated, stuck on the rocks and unable to get to the water. That would be sad, being that close to what it needed to live and unable to reach it.

She bent and peered at its face. It certainly was gross. Its large black eyes stared straight ahead. She jerked back. She could have sworn its eyes had adjusted but there were no whites just pupil so it was hard to tell. She stood still for several minutes but the creature didn't move. It must have been her imagination; it was certainly running wild today. She leaned in closer. Its mouth was wide open and filled with rows of long, sharp teeth. It smelled briny like the lake. Its lips quivered slightly and she jerked upright, stumbling backward and falling right next to it, within reach of its long arms.

She dropped the stick as she scrambled backward out of the water and sat panting on shore. It was alive. She was such an idiot to get so close. It lay half-in and half-out of the water, its head angled in an uncomfortable looking position. Was it in pain? She shook her head. What did that matter? She needed to go and this thing was not her problem. She stood and started to walk away. She sighed. If it was a bird or squirrel, even a mouse or rat, she'd help it without thinking twice. It wasn't the creature's fault that it was hairless and nasty looking and stinky.

She turned around and trudged over to it. If it were going to attack her it would have done it by now. She studied it closely. Two of the four slits on its side were moving a little. It was more of a slight tremble than an

44

actual movement. The other two were stuck firmly together. As the side slits shivered, the creature's bottom jaw moved forward and back. It was like the face Adam, her baby brother, had made once when he'd swallowed too much bread. That was it! The creature was choking. She quickly filled her bottle from the river. A fish couldn't breathe air. She dumped the water over its head and chest.

The fish-man made a slight coughing sound. She jerked upright but forced herself to stay put. It still was not moving. She wasn't in any danger. She filled up her jug again and poured it on the creature. It made another gasping sound.

She had to get it back into the water. She wrinkled her nose and placed both hands on its torso and shoved, trying to push it into the river without going any deeper into the water herself. It was cold to the touch and heavy. She tried again but it didn't budge. Maybe, she could give it enough water so that it could get a deep breath and move itself. She filled up her bottle again, emptying the contents over the gills. She continued this for several minutes, but the creature remained still. This obviously wasn't working.

The creature raised its arm, hitting her thigh. She flew out of the water, screeching. She shivered as she stood on the shore wiping at her leg to remove the memory of its clammy touch. Then its arm flapped again landing on its neck. Her face heated in embarrassment. It hadn't been reaching for her. She straightened her shoulders, took a deep breath and tromped back into the river. No matter what, she was going to help this thing.

The hand that had landed on its neck moved in a grasping fashion. She bit her lip and cautiously lifted the flipper between the tips of her fingers and moved it out of the way. There were two slashes on the creature's neck. They looked like the ones on its side except these were clogged full of…something. She grimaced as she dug her finger into a slit, pulling out mud and gunk. The foul stench of rotten vegetation and feces seeped out from the slime. She flung it into the water. She turned her head to the side, took a deep breath and held it. She dug into the second slit. When it was cleared a sharp intake of raspy breath came from the fish-man and then another.

She frowned. It was breathing air, but that didn't make sense. Fish breathed underwater. She dumped water on the two slits that she'd cleared. The creature choked and gasped. It rolled away from her and clambered onto its knees. It seemed larger and more dangerous now that it was mobile. She scurried back to the safety of the shore. The fish-man took several deep breaths and then slowly dragged itself back into the water, disappearing under the waves.

She stared at the surface, her heart racing. There was no sign of it. The river flowed without a ripple of disturbance aside from the motion of the water itself. The fish-man was gone. She smiled and began to walk again, her step a little lighter. She had saved its life. She glanced warily back at the water. She and Travis used to play in the river. She wouldn't be doing that again. If there were one of those things in there, there were more.

There was a slight rustle in the brush to her left. She jumped, turning to face the forest when a splash from the river drew her gaze. A flipper dipped under the water. Her shoulders sagged. *Great. Now, I'm being hunted by land and sea.* She moved a little away from the river but not too close to the forest. It was the best that she could do.

She continued on for another hour without a sound from the river or forest, which was encouraging. It was getting late. She was going to have to find somewhere to camp for the night. She shaded her eyes from the setting sun and groaned. She was an idiot. She'd been heading west. She should have been heading east. She must have gotten turned around in the thick underbrush. She started back the way she'd come. All this time had been wasted. An entire day was gone.

A mournful howling broke the silence of the forest. A shiver danced down her spine, raising the hair on her back. A cacophony of screeches and chirps echoed from the brush. Then there was silence, not a chirp or rustle to be heard. She swallowed around a lump in her throat. Whatever made that sound was close.

There was no movement or eyes shining back at her from the brush. She hurried along. A sharp yell pierced the air. She stumbled to a halt, tipping her head to better catch the sound. There was another shout. *Guards on scent.* Had the Almightys discovered her escape? No, that was impossible. It was probably just some Guards out hunting, but that didn't solve her problem. If she were caught, she would be in deep trouble.

She had to get out of there, but which way? To her left was the river. She swallowed. She hadn't seen the fishman for a while, but it didn't mean he wasn't lurking nearby. To her right were the woods. If something were following her, it was hiding in there. She glanced back and forth, undecided. The Guards might scare away the forest predator. She bolted into the trees. There was no way she was going to outrun them, so she had to hide.

She ran blindly away from the sound of the Guards, her backpack slamming against her spine with each stride. *If they catch my scent, they will find me.* She skidded to a stop. The forest had ended. A rock wall loomed in front of her, stretching to both sides as far as she could see. Little crevices and divots peppered the wall, but it was too steep to climb. She had to make a choice. The wrong one would cost her freedom, maybe her life.

The trees rustled behind her. *Too late. They found me.* This had all been for nothing. Now, the best she could hope for was to be taken with the others. Her chest tightened. She had to make sure that her mom and Remy weren't punished because she escaped. She raised her hands to her shoulders and slowly turned. Her breath caught in her throat. A Tracker, the deadliest of predators, stood on its back two legs, towering above her, front legs hanging down like arms. Brindle fur covered its body and its eyes glowed yellow in the shadowed forest. Its tongue lolled out the side of its mouth, exposing a row of sharp teeth on the other side. *Someone should tell it that they no longer exist in the wild.*

48

Grab your free copy now and find out what happens next.

https://books2read.com/u/31xPN7

Characters

Gillstrom: Micah's boss
Beth Lazetti: Bobby's sister (older)
Bobby Lazetti: The boy
Dad, Greg Lazetti: Bobby's father
Micah: An Angel of Death
Mom (Lazetti): Bobby 's mother
Nick Lazetti: Bobby's older brother
Ricky Lazetti: Bobby's younger brother

Author Bio

L. S. O'Dea grew up the youngest of seven in a family that uses teasing and tricks as an indication of love (or at least that's what she tells herself). Being five years younger than her closest sibling often made her the unwilling entertainment for her brothers and sisters.

Before she started kindergarten her brothers taught her how to spell her first and middle name—Linda Sue. She was so proud she ran into the kitchen to tell her mother. She stood tall and recited the letters of her name: L-E-M-O-N H-E-A-D.

She's pretty sure she has her siblings to thank for the demons that lurk in her mind, whispering dark and demented stories.

www.ingramcontent.com/pod-product-compliance
Lightning Source LLC
Chambersburg PA
CBHW070810120626
46557CB00002B/793